Ten in the Bed

Brita Granström

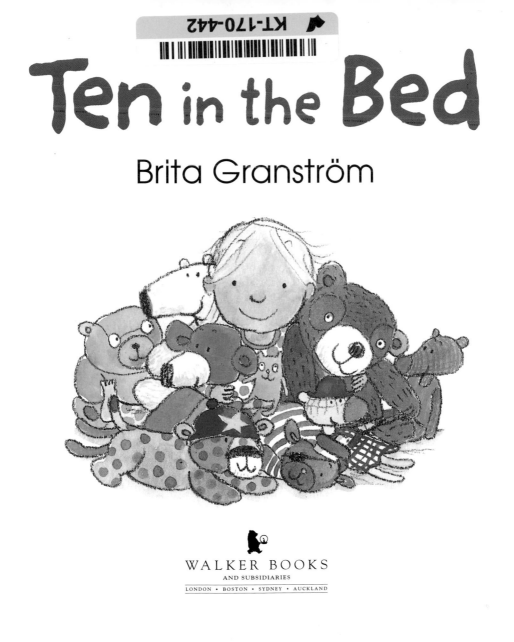

WALKER BOOKS
AND SUBSIDIARIES
LONDON · BOSTON · SYDNEY · AUCKLAND

There were ten in the bed
And the little one said,
"Roll over, roll over!"
So they all rolled over
And one fell out...
PLONK!

There were nine in the bed
And the little one said,
"Roll over, roll over!"
So they all rolled over
And one fell out...
PLONK!

There were eight in the bed
And the little one said,
"Roll over, roll over!"
So they all rolled over
And one fell out...

PLONK!

There were seven in the bed
And the little one said,
"Roll over, roll over!"
So they all rolled over
And one fell out...

PLONK!

There were six in the bed
And the little one said,
"Roll over, roll over!"
So they all rolled over
And one fell out...

PLONK!

There were five in the bed
And the little one said,
"Roll over, roll over!"
So they all rolled over
And one fell out... PLONK!

There were four in the bed
And the little one said,
"Roll over, roll over!"
So they all rolled over
And one fell out...
PLONK!

There were three in the bed
And the little one said,
"Roll over, roll over!"
So they all rolled over
And one fell out...

PLONK!

There were two in the bed
And the little one said,
"Roll over, roll over!"
So they all rolled over
And one fell out...
PLONK!

There was one
left in the bed,
The little one,
who said...

"Come back
to bed!"

To Mick and Charlotte with love
B.G.

First published 1996 by Walker Books Ltd
87 Vauxhall Walk, London SE11 5HJ
This edition published 2009
2 4 6 8 10 9 7 5 3 1
Illustrations © 1996 Brita Granström
The right of Brita Granström to be identified as illustrator of this work has been
asserted by her in accordance with the Copyright, Designs and Patents Act 1988
This book has been typeset in Joe Overweight
Printed in China
British Library Cataloguing in Publication Data:
a catalogue record for this book is available from the British Library.
ISBN 978-0-7445-3963-9
www.walker.co.uk